Tunnel King

Dave and Pat Sargent are longtime residents of Prairie Grove, Arkansas. Dave, a fourth-generation dairy farmer, began writing in early December of 1990, and Pat, a former teacher, began writing in the fourth grade. They enjoy the outdoors and have a real love for animals.

Tunnel King

Animal Pride Series
Book 11

By

Dave and Pat Sargent

Beyond The End
By
Sue Rogers

Illustrated by
Jeane Lirley Huff

Ozark Publishing, Inc.
P.O. Box 228
Prairie Grove, AR 72753

Cataloging-in-Publication Data

Sargent, Dave, 1941-
    Tunnel King / by Dave and Pat Sargent ; illustrated
by Jeane Lirley Huff. —Prairie Grove, AR : Ozark
Publishing, ©2003.
        ix, 36 p. : col. ill. ; 21 cm. (Animal pride series ; 11)
        "I work hard"—Cover.
        SUMMARY: A young gopher comes to the rescue
when his family becomes trapped underground.
Includes facts about the physical characteristics,
behavior, habitat, and predators of the gopher.
        ISBN: 1-56763-779-5 (hc)
                 1-56763-780-9 (pbk)
        1. Pocket gophers—Juvenile fiction. [1. Gophers—
Fiction.] I. Sargent, Pat, 1936- II. Huff, Jeane Lirley,
1946- ill. III. Title. IV. Series: Sargent, Dave, 1941-
Animal pride series ; 11.

        PZ10.3.S243Tu 2003
        [Fic]—dc21   96-001497

Factual information excerpted/adapted from
THE WORLD BOOK ENCYCLOPEDIA.
© World Book, Inc. By permission of the publisher.
www.worldbook.com

Printed in the United States of America

iv

Inspired by

a family of gophers that live on our farm.

Dedicated to

my good buddy, Andrew Happy.

Foreword

A gopher family gets trapped in its den. When Little Tom saves them, he becomes known as "The Tunnel King".

Contents

If you would like to have the authors of the Animal Pride Series visit your school, free of charge, call 1-800-321-5671 or 1-800-960-3876.

One

A New Playground

One warm spring morning the gopher family was awakened by Farmer John's noisy tractor. They had just moved into a new den and had spent several days digging it out and getting it ready. The ground was very hard, and there were lots of roots from nearby trees that made the digging hard and slow.

Farmer John had noticed the gopher's entrance and knew they were living in a den underground. He didn't really pay them any mind

1

because he knew that gophers had several entrances to their dens and covering up one wouldn't bother them at all. But what Farmer John didn't know was that this entrance was the only one they had.

Farmer John had to build a new hay barn before hay-cutting time, and this was the best spot for it. He kept scraping the top of the ground with the blade on his tractor, trying to get the ground level enough to pour a concrete floor for the barn.

It was noon before Farmer John stopped scraping the ground with that noisy tractor. He then went home for lunch.

When the gophers could no longer hear the tractor, they scurried out of their den through the entrance to see what had been going on.

When the gophers got outside, all they could see was bare ground. Farmer John had scraped every bit of the grass away. The gophers thought the fresh, moist dirt was their new playground. They had fun playing gopher games on the new pad.

Suddenly, Mama Gopher stood up on her back legs and sounded the alarm. They stopped and listened. It was that noisy tractor coming back! The gophers ran for their tunnel and one by one disappeared underground.

When Farmer John got there, he began scraping the ground again with the blade. He had to get the pad just right.

The noise from the tractor and the loud scraping sound went on all afternoon. It was sundown when Farmer John headed to the house on his tractor.

Once again, the gopher family scampered from the den to check out their new playground. Why, it was as smooth and level as it could be. The gophers played in the loose fluffy dirt until dark.

Early the next morning the gopher family was awakened by a loud hammering sound, and they could feel the ground vibrating. Daddy Gopher stuck his head out of the tunnel to see what was going on.

Daddy Gopher was amazed! Farmer John was building a frame around their new playground. He was using a big hammer to drive stakes into the ground to hold the frame up.

Daddy Gopher ducked back into the den and told the others how nice Farmer John was to fix up their new playground.

There were five in the gopher family. There were Daddy Gopher and Mama Gopher. And there were three youngsters, Mike, Joe, and Little Tom. Little Tom was called Little Tom because of his size. He was the smallest of the three youngsters.

Being the smallest made life a lot rougher for Little Tom. Mike and Joe were always pushing him around and making fun of him. He tried to fight back, but Mike and Joe were too strong.

When the sun was high in the sky, Farmer John went to the house to eat. The gophers checked out the frame around the new playground.

Farmer John had been gone for only a short while when Little Tom spotted him heading their way again. He called to the others and ran down the hole, followed closely by the rest of the family.

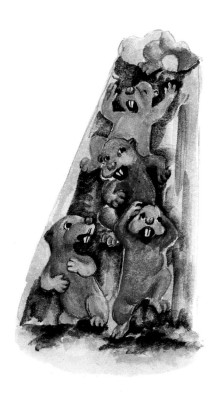

For a couple of hours, all kinds of strange noises could be heard. Around mid-afternoon that day, everything went black.

Farmer John had blocked their tunnel entrance again. Since he had done the same thing two or three times before, the gophers didn't think it was a problem. They would dig out again when Farmer John left.

Two

The Concrete Slab

By late afternoon the noise and vibrations stopped. Daddy Gopher made his way to the tunnel entrance and began digging at it. It was like a rock! He couldn't break it up at all.

Farmer John had poured a big concrete slab right over the top of the gophers' den. The concrete slab would be the floor for his new hay barn. The gophers could not dig through the concrete, and there was no other entrance to their new den. Without air, they would suffocate.

11

Daddy Gopher kept digging at the hard concrete, but it was no use. He could not dig through. He finally decided to dig along the bottom of the concrete until he reached the edge, and then tunnel up. So he started digging along the top of the ground just under the concrete.

Daddy Gopher could dig only a very little dirt now, for his claws, which he used for digging, were worn down to the quick. They throbbed and ached and then started to bleed. He could dig no more. It looked as if they were doomed.

Mama Gopher said she would try digging a tunnel to the outside. She took a deep breath and started digging. The ground was packed hard and the digging was extremely slow.

Mama Gopher dug and dug and dug, and after three long hours, she had dug only three feet. She knew that if she could dig only a foot each hour, they would never be able to get out before they ran out of air, and they would all die.

But Mama Gopher continued digging as hard and as fast as she could. She dug another foot, then ran into a giant rock. She dug to the right, but could not find a way around it. Then she dug to the left. She dug and dug, but she could not find a way around the giant rock.

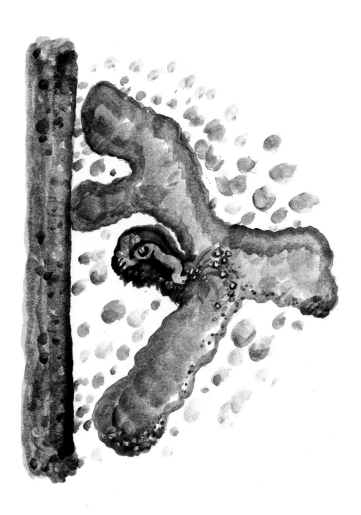

Daddy Gopher told her to try digging under the rock. So now, Mama Gopher dug down, trying to find the bottom of the rock. She dug a hole four feet deep and still could not find the bottom of the rock. She stopped and told the family it was no use. She could not find a way out.

They thought and thought, then decided to dig in a new direction.

Daddy Gopher said, "Mike, you start digging in the direction of Farmer John's house. You dig for a while then let Joe dig for a little while. Then, your mama can dig again. If you all take turns, you should be able to dig out in a couple of hours. I'll keep the dirt moved out of the way."

"But what about me, Daddy?" asked Tom. "Don't I get a turn?"

Daddy Gopher sort of chuckled and said, "Oh, you're too small, son. You would only get in the way."

"Yeah," teased Mike. "Why don't you just step back out of the way and let us big boys do the work, Little Tom. Like Daddy said, you're too little to help."

Joe had to put in his two cents' worth. He said, "Watch me when it comes my turn to dig, and I'll show you how it's really done."

Little Tom crawled back to the far corner of the den and lay down.

"Why don't they ever let me do something?" he said. "I bet I could dig faster and farther than anyone if they'd just let me."

Little Tom could hear the others as they took turns digging. Then he said, "I'll dig a tunnel of my own!" He started a tunnel on the backside of the den. He dug in the opposite direction from the others.

18

Mama Gopher, Mike, and Joe were getting very tired and were having lots of problems. They kept running into rocks. They had to dig around the big rocks and move the smaller ones out of the way.

No one noticed that Little Tom was gone. They were far too busy digging and moving dirt.

Little Tom was busy digging, too. He was having fun and was happy.

It was Mama Gopher's turn to dig. She dug furiously at the rocky ground. The rocks were not big, but they were hard on Mama Gopher's claws.

Mama Gopher's paws were sore, and she found the digging almost impossible. Every time she tried to dig, her paws hurt so badly she had to quit.

Daddy Gopher told Mike and Joe that it was up to them to save the family. Mama Gopher's paws were bruised and cut so much from the rocks that she could no longer dig.

Three

Tom Digs a Tunnel

Mike and Joe now took turns digging. They knew that everyone depended on them.

When it came Mike's turn to dig, he clawed away at the dirt. They had gotten past the rocks, and the digging was much easier and going much faster now. Everything looked good, and they thought they would be out in just a little while.

Mike started getting real tired, so Joe took over. Joe, thinking they would soon be out, dug like crazy.

He was really moving a lot of dirt when, all of a sudden, he screamed.

Mama Gopher called out, "Oh, dear me! What happened, Joe?"

"I cut my paw on a jagged rock and it hurts bad! It's bleeding, too!" he added.

"Come on out and let Mike dig for a while," Mama Gopher said. "I'll take a look at your paw."

Joe backed out of the tunnel and, while Mama Gopher checked his paw, Mike crawled back into the tunnel and began digging.

Mama Gopher looked at Joe's poor little paw. He had caught one of his claws on the sharp edge of a jagged rock and had torn the claw completely off. Joe wouldn't be able to dig anymore. Now it was all up to Mike.

Mama Gopher told Joe it would take about three weeks for him to grow a new claw. She told him he would have to be real careful for a couple of days and keep it clean.

Mike got tired and had to stop for a while. He backed out of the tunnel and curled up in a ball to rest for a few minutes.

Everyone was getting weak. The oxygen in the air was almost gone. They knew that if Mike didn't reach the outside soon, it would be too late.

Mama Gopher looked at Mike. He was so tired he had drifted off to sleep. Mama Gopher woke him up and told him he would have to go back to digging. She told him that there was only enough air left to last for maybe one hour.

Mike went back to digging, but it was slow and hard, and he was very tired. He had been digging for about thirty minutes before he backed out of the tunnel and told the others that it was no use. He said he had run into rocks again, and didn't have the strength to dig through.

They sat and talked for a few minutes, trying to figure out what to do. Then Mama Gopher said, "Tom! We'll let Little Tom dig for awhile!"

Daddy Gopher spoke up and said, "You can forget about Tom. He's much too small, and he's not strong enough to dig a tunnel."

"But Tom is our only chance," Mama Gopher snapped. "Without him, we'll all die!"

"Well, I guess it won't hurt to give him a chance," Daddy Gopher replied.

Mama Gopher called, "Tom! Come here, Little Tom! We need your help!" There was no answer.

"It's not like Little Tom to not answer me," Mama Gopher said.

"The little fellow is probably asleep," Daddy Gopher replied.

"Let's see if we can find him," Mama Gopher ordered.

Everyone started looking for Little Tom, but Tom was nowhere to be found.

"He may be back in one of the dead-end tunnels that we've filled with dirt," Joe said.

Mama Gopher said sadly, "Poor Little Tom is gone. I just know he's been buried in one of the tunnels."

The gophers were getting weak. Mike and Joe had fallen asleep, and Daddy Gopher and Mama Gopher slowly collapsed. The air was gone. The gophers were dying.

Suddenly, there was a barking sound and fresh air could be felt flowing through the den. When the gophers breathed the fresh air, they started waking up. They saw light. Then, they saw Little Tom standing next to the tunnel he had dug.

Little Tom had dug a tunnel to the surface, all by himself. The exhausted gopher family crawled to the outside through Little Tom's new tunnel.

Mike and Joe never picked on Little Tom anymore. In fact, they treated him with respect. And of course, they dropped the word *Little*.

Tom became known to all the gophers all over the farm as the Tunnel King.

Four

Gopher Facts

The gopher is a small mammal that lives in underground tunnels.

Gophers dig the tunnels with the large claws of their front feet and with their front teeth.

Gophers move slow and spend most of their time alone in the dark tunnels, which may be as long as eight hundred feet. They keep other gophers from entering the tunnels, except in the breeding season.

Gophers live in all regions of North America, except the far north and the east. They are also called pocket gophers because they have fur-lined pouches on the outsides of their cheeks.

Pocket gophers grow about ten inches long. They have short legs, a broad blunt head, small ears and eyes, and a short tail. Their nearly hairless tail is tactile. That is, it serves as an organ of touch. They feel their way with the tail when they back up in a tunnel.

Gophers usually vary in color from reddish brown to slate gray. They eat buds, farm vegetables, grass, nuts, and roots. They carry food in their cheek pouches.

The digging of gophers breaks up tightly packed soil and thus can help promote the growth of plants. Gophers are rodents and belong to the same order as beavers, mice, and squirrels.

BEYOND "THE END" . . .

LANGUAGE LINKS

When we describe ourselves to someone who doesn't know us, we usually are very honest and reveal how we feel about ourselves. Pretend to be Little Tom, the smallest gopher who got pushed around and was made fun of. Two days before the gopher family's almost tragic accident, Little Tom's new teacher was trying to get to know her students before the first day of school. She asked Little Tom to write her a short introduction of himself. Write an introduction as though you are Little Tom and describe how you feel about yourself.

Now it is two days after the scary experience for the gopher family. You, Little Tom (now known as Tunnel King), have saved your entire family. Write a new introduction describing yourself!

In both descriptions, use as many details as possible. Begin with, "Hello, I am a gopher." Make it interesting!

CURRICULUM LINKS

How does a gopher know how to dig tunnels? Work in groups to research gophers. One group finds what gophers eat; group two finds the habitat of gophers; and the third group finds the behaviors of gophers. Each group writes a brief description of its findings. Once the reports are given, the class can make a drawing of a gopher and discuss how the animal's physical characteristics and instinctual behaviors contribute to digging tunnels.

Create a list of ten of your individual behaviors, such as waking up, brushing your teeth, walking, eating, or reading. Which of these are learned? Which are instincts? If they were learned, how did you learn them?

Children are fascinated with the subject of hibernation, so a discussion of animal instincts usually leads to hibernation. Go to this web site, "How Do Animals Spend the Winter?" for good information on hibernation and migration: <www.sciencemadesimple.com/animals.html>.

Man makes tunnels also. Is this a learned behavior or an instinctual behavior? Engineers have recently designed and built The Ted Williams Tunnel in Boston, Massachusetts. The total length of this tunnel is 1.6 miles. It is a road tunnel beneath South Boston and Boston Harbor.